KU-424-806

To Jimmy and Jumper!

from Lindsey and Lola x

OXFORD
UNIVERSITY PRESS

Great Clarendon Street, Oxford OX2 6DP

Oxford University Press is a department of the University of Oxford.
It furthers the University's objective of excellence in research, scholarship,
and education by publishing worldwide in

Oxford   New York

Auckland   Cape Town   Dar es Salaam   Hong Kong   Karachi
Kuala Lumpur   Madrid   Melbourne   Mexico City   Nairobi
New Delhi   Shanghai   Taipei   Toronto

With offices in

Argentina   Austria   Brazil   Chile   Czech Republic   France   Greece
Guatemala   Hungary   Italy   Japan   Poland   Portugal   Singapore
South Korea   Switzerland   Thailand   Turkey   Ukraine   Vietnam

Oxford is a registered trade mark of Oxford University Press
in the UK and in certain other countries

Database right Oxford University Press (maker)

First published 2006

British Library Cataloguing in Publication Data available

ISBN-13: 978-0-19-279166-5 (Hardback)
ISBN-10: 0-19-279166-4 (Hardback)

ISBN-13: 978-0-19-279167-2 (Paperback)
ISBN-10: 0-19-279167-2 (Paperback)

10 9 8 7 6 5 4 3 2 1

Printed in Singapore

Boing...

People say I'm really cute.

First they say, 'You're so sweet, LOLA.'

Then they say,
'Would you like a TREAT, Lola?'

It can be hard
to say 'NO'

and, anyway,
it would be rude to refuse . . . wouldn't it?

So I eat lots and lots of TREATS!

Sometimes I find myself **slumped** by the fridge having **A MIDNIGHT FEAST.**

When I can't SQUEEZE into my kennel, Marcie smiles, 'Maybe you shouldn't have emptied the fridge last night, Lola.'

LoLA

And when I can't climb onto my **FAVOURITE** chair for a nap,

Marcie decides something **mUst** be done.

So we go to the park.
'For some **EXERCISE**,' says Marcie.

I spot Freckles on the
seesaw and I plump
myself down . . .

But I prefer to ride on Marcie's skateboard!

Sending her FLYING into the bushes.

Ooops!

We're just picking the flowers off Freckles,
when suddenly
there's lots of BARKING and YAPPING.

And before you can say

JAMMY DOUGHNUTS
Bandit, Darma and Jumper
whoosh past us.

Marcie and Freckles start running, too, leaving me to catch up.

At last, I see what all the fuss is about.

A new doggy playground!

Pablo and Murray . . .

Bandit and Jumper . . .

Darma and Freckles . . .

are having BAGS of fun! I want to join in.

But it's not as much FUN as I thought.
Especially with everyone yelling at me!

'UP, Lola!'

'PUSH, Lola!'

'GO, Lola!'

'JUMP, Lola!'

'Come on, Lola!'

'OVER, Lola,
not under!'

'Keep going!' Marcie shouts.
But I can't . . . so I stay in the tunnel.

I just want
to **HIDE**.

In the morning Marcie is full of beans. 'We're going to get **FIT!**' she says.

And **ONE** and **TWO** and **THREE** . . .

the MARKET!'
It's full of LOTS and

LOTS of the juiciest treats.

Who needs chocolate cake after all?

Now I can **leap** onto my favourite chair . . .

SUCCESS!

I must be getting fitter.

'COME ON, Marcie!' I say.
'We're slimmer, we're trimmer
and we're ready for the doggy playground!'

And I DO.

There are treats all round and before you can say **Strawberry cheesecake,**

we all **TUCK** in.